W. Stanley

Instructions for Using a Slide Rule

W. Stanley

Instructions for Using a Slide Rule

Instructions for Using a Slide Rule

by W. Stanley

CONTENTS

INSTRUCTIONS FOR USING A SLIDE RULE	1
DESCRIPTION OF A SLIDE RULE	3
MULTIPLICATION	5
METHOD OF MAKING SETTINGS	7
DIVISION	17
THE CI SCALE	27
SQUARING AND SQUARE ROOT	29
CUBING AND CUBE ROOT	43
THE 1.5 AND 2/3 POWER	57
COMBINATIONS OF PROCESSES	59
PRACTICAL PROBLEMS SOLVED BY SLIDE RULE	63
CONVERSION FACTORS	65

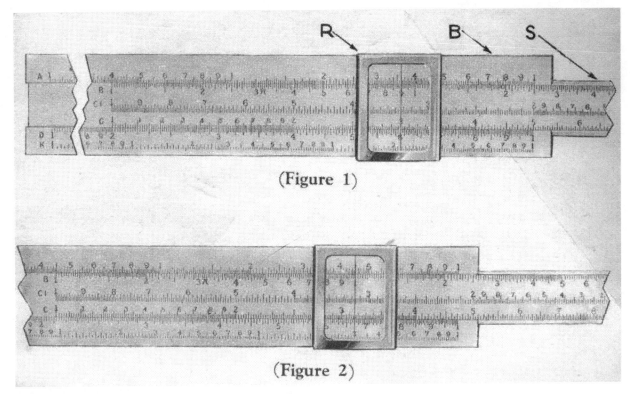

(Figure 1)

(Figure 2)

INSTRUCTIONS FOR USING A SLIDE RULE

The slide rule is a device for easily and quickly multiplying, dividing and extracting square root and cube root. It will also perform any combination of these processes. On this account, it is found extremely useful by students and teachers in schools and colleges, by engineers, architects, draftsmen, surveyors, chemists, and many others. Accountants and clerks find it very helpful when approximate calculations must be made rapidly. The operation of a slide rule is extremely easy, and it is well worth while for anyone who is called upon to do much numerical calculation to learn to use one. It is the purpose of this manual to explain the operation in such a way that a person who has never before used a slide rule may teach himself to do so.

DESCRIPTION OF SLIDE RULE

The slide rule consists of three parts (see figure 1). B is the body of the rule and carries three scales marked A, D and K. S is the slider which moves relative to the body and also carries three scales marked B, CI and C. R is the runner or indicator and is marked in the center with a hair-line. The scales A and B are identical and are used in problems involving square root. Scales C and D are also identical and are used for multiplication and division. Scale K is for finding cube root. Scale CI, or C-inverse, is like scale C except that it is laid off from right to left instead of from left to right. It is useful in problems involving reciprocals.

MULTIPLICATION

We will start with a very simple example:

Example 1: 2 * 3 = 6

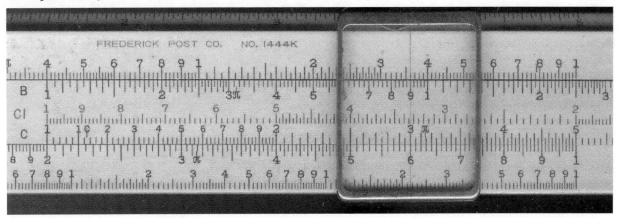

To prove this on the slide rule, move the slider so that the 1 at the left-hand end of the C scale is directly over the large 2 on the D scale (see figure 1). Then move the runner till the hair-line is over 3 on the C scale. Read the answer, 6, on the D scale under the hair-line. Now, let us consider a more complicated example:

Example 2:   2.12 * 3.16 = 6.70

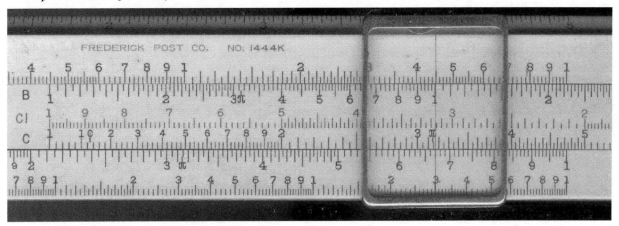

As before, set the 1 at the left-hand end of the C scale, which we will call the left-hand index of the C scale, over 2.12 on the D scale (See figure 2). The hair-line of the runner is now placed over 3.16 on the C scale and the answer, 6.70, read on the D scale.

METHOD OF MAKING SETTINGS

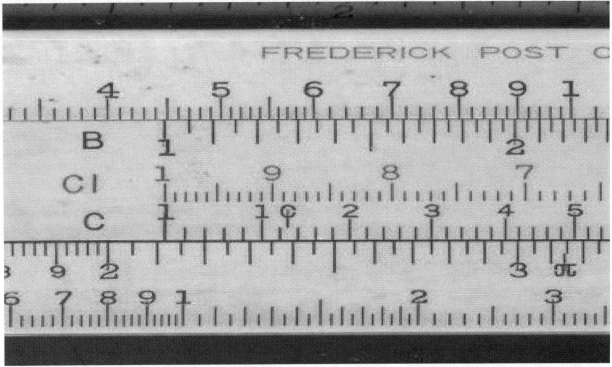

[This 6 inch rule uses fewer minor divisions.]

In order to understand just why 2.12 is set where it is (figure 2), notice that the interval from 2 to 3 is divided into 10 large or major divisions, each of which is, of course, equal to one-tenth (0.1) of the amount represented by the whole interval. The major divisions are in turn divided into 5 small or minor divisions, each of which is one-fifth or two-tenths (0.2) of the major division, that is 0.02 of the whole interval. Therefore, the index is set above

2 + 1 major division + 1 minor division = 2 + 0.1 + 0.02 = 2.12.

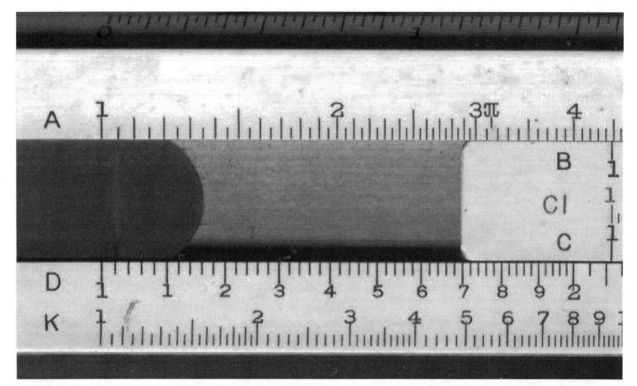

In the same way we find 3.16 on the C scale. While we are on this subject, notice that in the interval from 1 to 2 the major divisions are marked with the small figures 1 to 9 and the minor divisions are 0.1 of the major divisions. In the intervals from 2 to 3 and 3 to 4 the minor divisions are 0.2 of the major divisions, and for the rest of the D (or C) scale, the minor divisions are 0.5 of the major divisions.

Reading the setting from a slide rule is very much like reading measurements from a ruler. Imagine that the divisions between 2 and 3 on the D scale (figure 2) are those of a ruler divided into tenths of a foot, and each tenth of a foot divided in 5 parts 0.02 of a foot long. Then the distance from one on the left-hand end of the D scale (not shown in figure 2) to one on the left-hand end of the C scale would he 2.12 feet. Of course, a foot rule is divided into parts of uniform length, while those on a slide rule get smaller toward the right-hand end, but this example may help to give an idea of the method of making and reading settings. Now consider another example.

Example 3a: 2.12 * 7.35 = 15.6

If we set the left-hand index of the C scale over 2.12 as in the last example, we find that 7.35 on the C scale falls out beyond the body of the rule. In a case like this, simply use the right-hand index of the C scale. If we set this over 2.12 on the D scale and move the runner to 7.35 on the C scale we read the result 15.6 on the D scale under the hair-line.

Now, the question immediately arises, why did we call the result 15.6 and not 1.56? The answer is that the slide rule takes no account of decimal points. Thus, the settings would be identical for all of the following products:

Example 3: a: 2.12 * 7.35 = 15.6 b: 21.2 * 7.35 = 156.0 c: 212 * 73.5 = 15600.
d: 2.12 * .0735 = .156 e: .00212 * 735 = .0156

The most convenient way to locate the decimal point is to make a mental multiplication using only the first digits in the given factors. Then place the decimal point in the slide rule result so that its value is nearest that of the mental multiplication. Thus, in example 3a above, we can multiply 2 by 7 in our heads and see immediately that the decimal point must be placed in the slide rule result 156 so that it becomes 15.6 which is nearest to 14. In example 3b (20 * 7 = 140), so we must place the decimal point to give 156. The reader can readily verify the other examples in the same way.

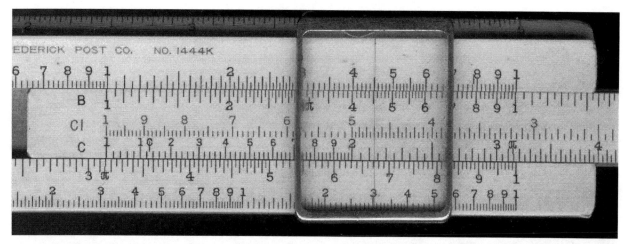

Since the product of a number by a second number is the same as the product of the second by the first, it makes no difference which of the two numbers is set first on the slide rule. Thus, an alternative way of working example 2 would be to set the left-hand index of the C scale over 3.16 on the D scale and move the runner to 2.12 on the C scale and read the answer under the hair-line on the D scale.

The A and B scales are made up of two identical halves each of which is very similar to the C and D scales. Multiplication can also be carried out on either half of the A and B scales exactly as it is done on the C and D scales. However, since the A and B scales are only half as long as the C and D scales, the accuracy is not as good. It is sometimes convenient to multiply on the A and B scales in more complicated problems as we shall see later on.

A group of examples follow which cover all the possible combination of settings which can arise in the multiplication of two numbers.

Example

4: 20 * 3 = 60

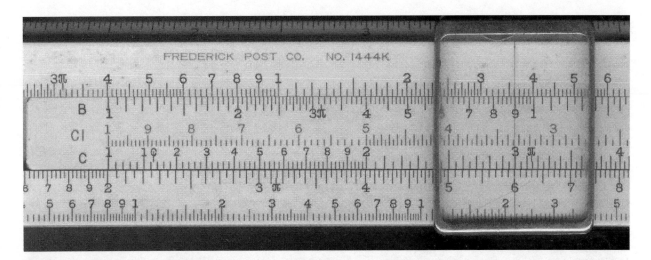

5: 85 * 2 = 170

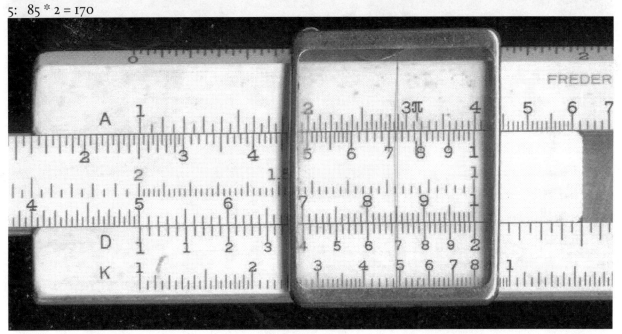

6: 45 * 35 = 1575

7: 151 * 42 = 6342

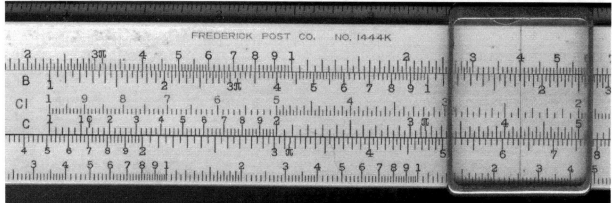

8: 6.5 * 15 = 97.5

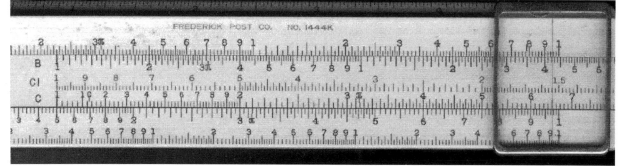

9: .34 * .08 = .0272

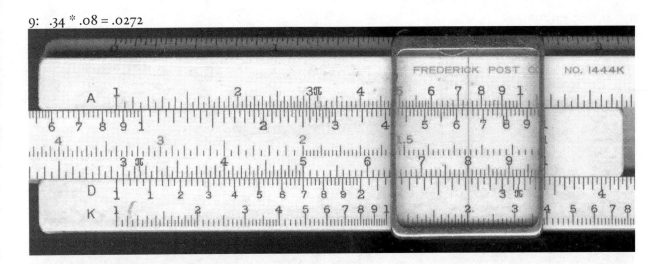

10: 75 * 26 = 1950

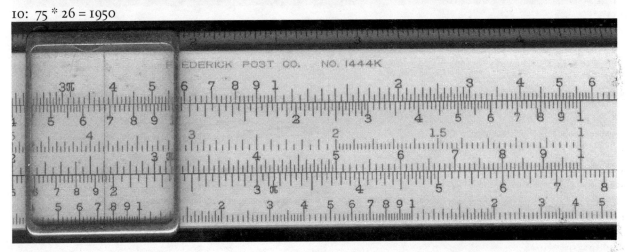

11: .00054 * 1.4 = .000756

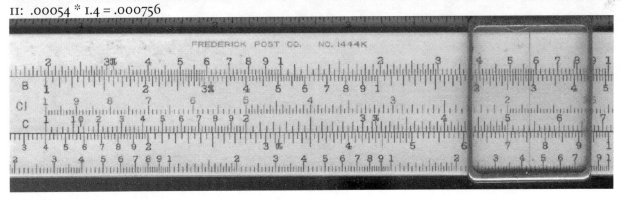

I2: 11.1 * 2.7 = 29.97

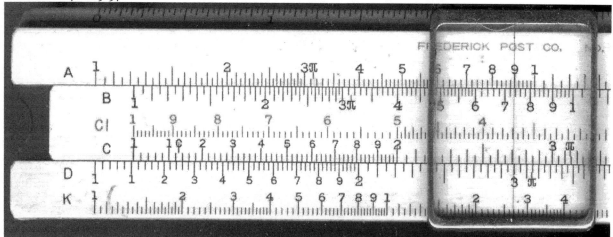

I3: 1.01 * 54 = 54.5

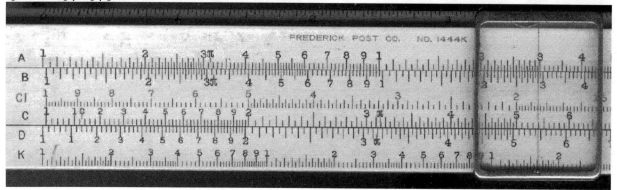

14: 3.14 * 25 = 78.5

DIVISION

Since multiplication and division are inverse processes, division on a slide rule is done by making the same settings as for multiplication, but in reverse order. Suppose we have the example:

Example 15: (6.70 / 2.12) = 3.16

Set indicator over the dividend 6.70 on the D scale. Move the slider until the divisor 2.12 on the C scale is under the hair-line. Then read the result on the D scale under the left-hand index of the C scale. As in multiplication, the decimal point must be placed by a separate process. Make all the digits except the first in both dividend and divisor equal zero and mentally divide the resulting numbers. Place the decimal point in the slide rule result so that it is nearest to the mental result. In example 15, we mentally divide 6 by 2. Then we place the decimal point in the slide rule result 316 so that it is 3.16 which is nearest to 3.

A group of examples for practice in division follow:

Example 16: 34 / 2 = 17

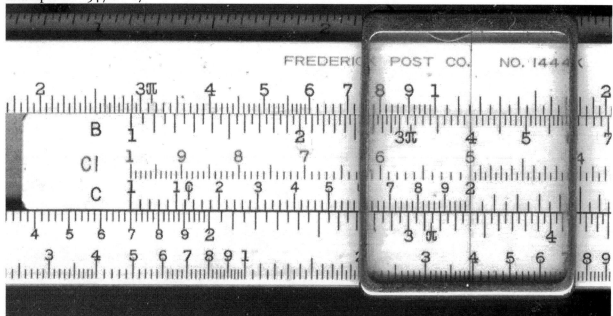

17: 49 / 7 = 7

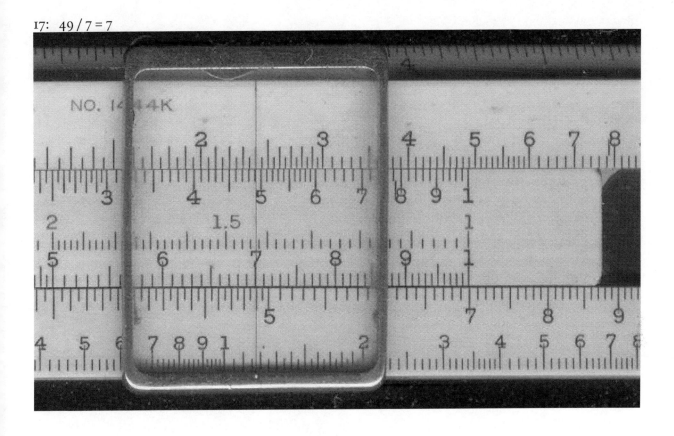

18: 132 / 12 = 11

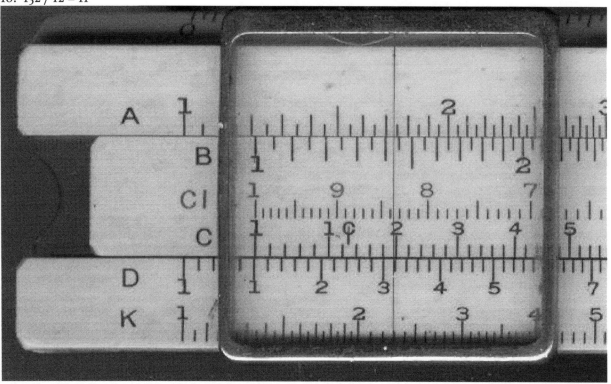

19: 480 / 16 = 30

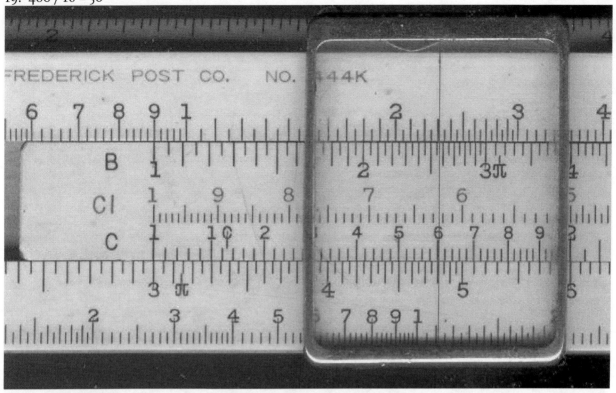

20: 1.05 / 35 = .03

21: 4.32 / 12 = .36

22: 5.23 / 6.15 = .85

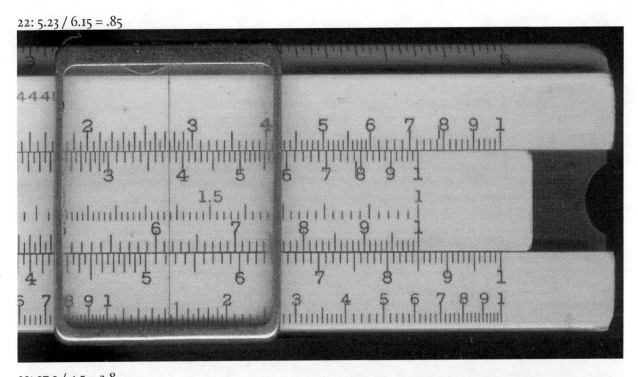

23: 17.1 / 4.5 = 3.8

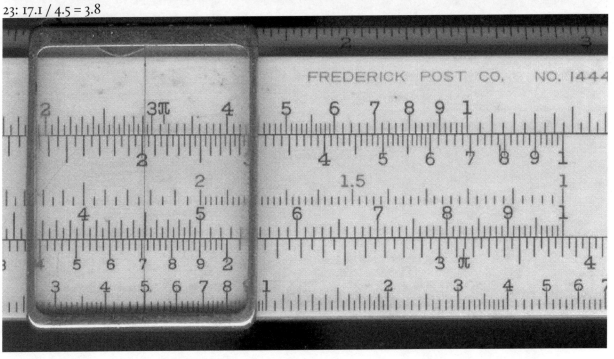

24: 1895 / 6.06 = 313

25: 45 / .017 = 2647

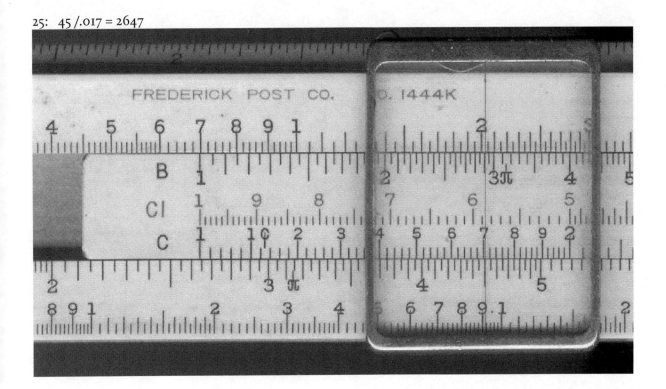

THE CI SCALE

If we divide one (1) by any number the answer is called the reciprocal of the number. Thus, one-half is the reciprocal of two, one-quarter is the reciprocal of four. If we take any number, say 14, and multiply it by the reciprocal of another number, say 2, we get:

Example 26: 14 * (1/2) = 7

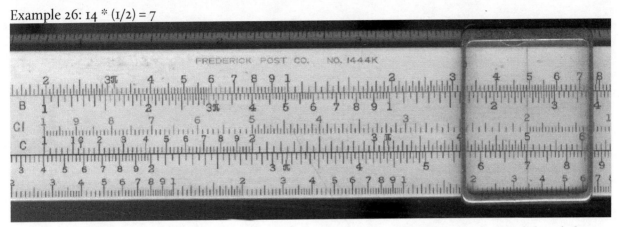

which is the same as 14 divided by two. This process can be carried out directly on the slide rule by use of the CI scale. Numbers on the CI scale are reciprocals of those on the C scale. Thus we see that 2 on the CI scale comes directly over 0.5 or 1/2 on the C scale. Similarly 4 on the CI scale comes over 0.25 or 1/4 on the C scale, and so on. To do example 26 by use of the CI scale, proceed exactly as if you were going to multiply in the usual manner except that you use the CI scale instead of the C scale. First set the left-hand index of the C scale over 14 on the D scale. Then move the indicator to 2 on the CI scale. Read the result, 7, on the D scale under the hair-line. This is really another way of dividing. THE READER IS ADVISED TO WORK EXAMPLES 16 TO 25 OVER AGAIN BY USE OF THE CI SCALE.

SQUARING AND SQUARE ROOT

If we take a number and multiply it by itself we call the result the square of the number. The process is called squaring the number. If we find the number which, when multiplied by itself is equal to a given number, the former number is called the square root of the given number. The process is called extracting the square root of the number. Both these processes may be carried out on the A and D scales of a slide rule. For example:

Example 27: 4 * 4 = square(4) = 16

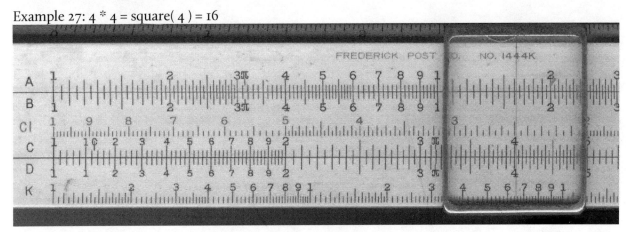

Set indicator over 4 on D scale. Read 16 on A scale under hair-line.

Example 28: square(25.4) = 646.0

The decimal point must be placed by mental survey. We know that square(25.4) must be a little larger than square(25) = 625 so that it must be 646.0.

To extract a square root, we set the indicator over the number on the A scale and read the result under the hair-line on the D scale. When we examine the A scale we see that there are two places where any given number may be set, so we must have some way of deciding in a given case which half of the A scale to use. The rule is as follows:

(a) If the number is greater than one. For an odd number of digits to the left of the decimal point, use the left-hand half of the A scale. For an even number of digits to the left of the decimal point, use the right-hand half of the A scale.

(b) If the number is less than one. For an odd number of zeros to the right of the decimal point before the first digit not a zero, use the left-hand half of the A scale. For none or any even number of zeros to the right of the decimal point before the first digit not a zero, use the right-hand half of the A scale.

Example 29: square_root(157) = 12.5

Since we have an odd number of digits set indicator over 157 on left-hand half of A scale. Read 12.5 on the D scale under hair-line. To check the decimal point think of the perfect square nearest to 157. It is 12 * 12 = 144, so that square_root(157) must be a little more than 12 or 12.5.

Example 30: square_root(.0037) = .0608

In this number we have an even number of zeros to the right of the decimal point, so we must set the indicator over 37 on the right-hand half of the A scale. Read 608 under the hair-line on D scale. To place the decimal point write:

square_root(.0037) = square_root(37/10000)   = 1/100 square_root(37)

The nearest perfect square to 37 is 6 * 6 = 36, so the answer should be a little more than 0.06 or .0608. All of what has been said about use of the A and D scales for squaring and extracting square root applies equally well to the B and C scales since they are identical to the A and D scales respectively.

A number of examples follow for squaring and the extraction of square root.

Example 31: square(2) = 4

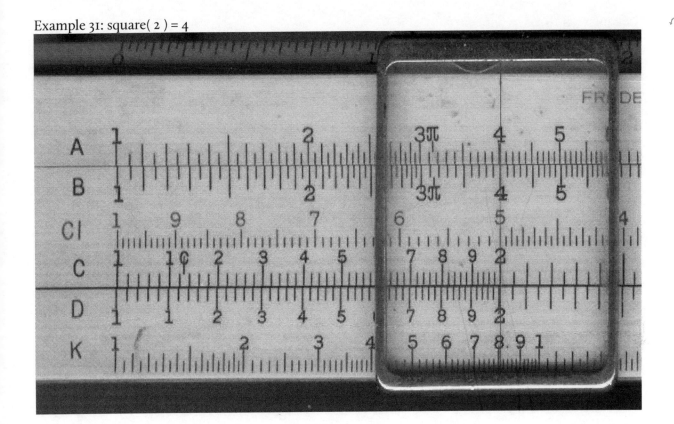

32: square(15) = 225

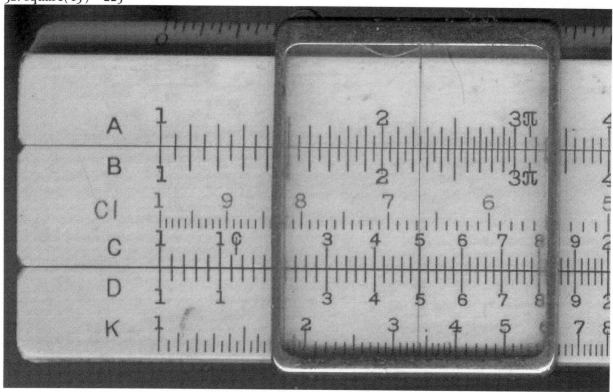

33: square(26) = 676

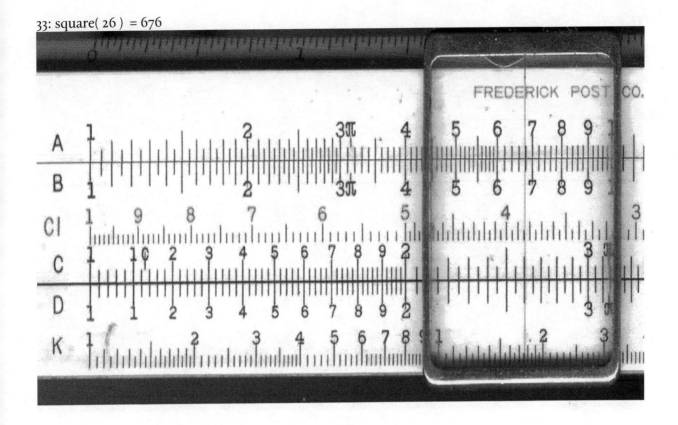

34: square(19.65) = 386

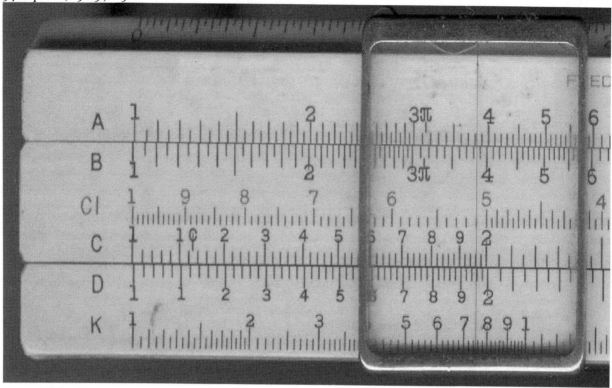

35: square_root(64) = 8

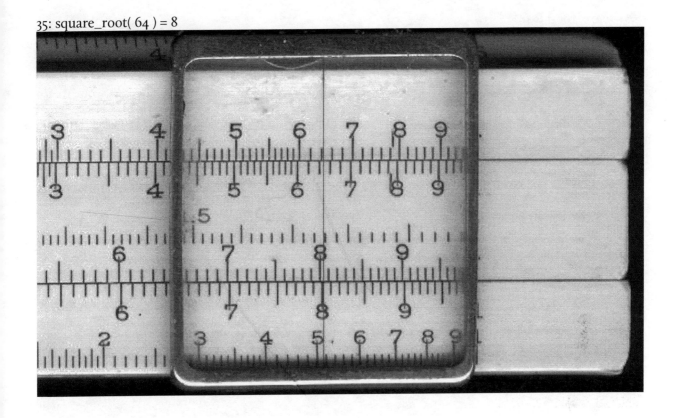

36: square_root(6.4) = 2.53

37: square_root(498) = 22.5

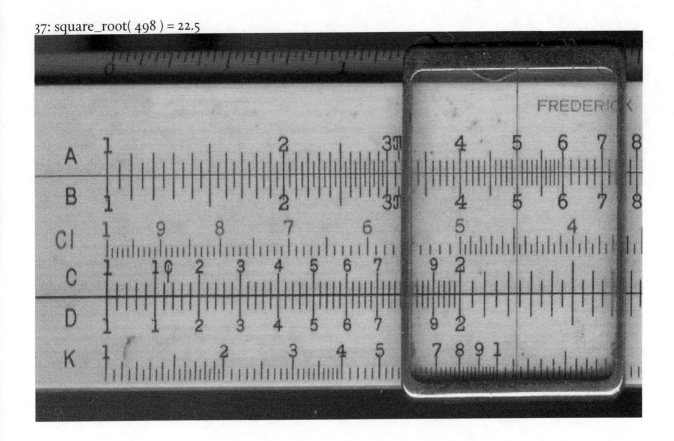

38: square_root(2500) = 50

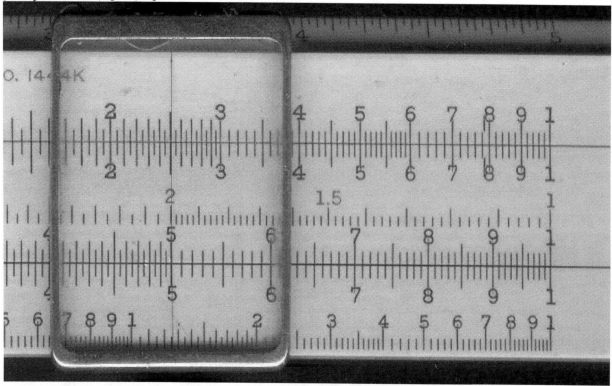

39: square_root(.16) = .04

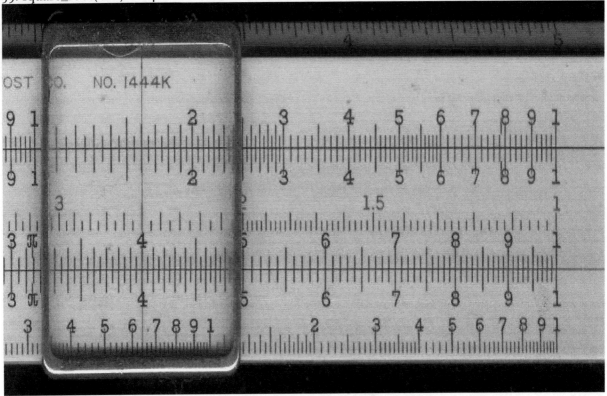

40: square_root(.03) = .173

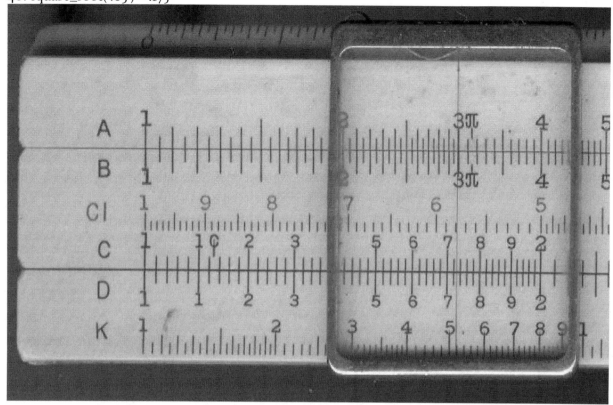

CUBING AND CUBE ROOT

If we take a number and multiply it by itself, and then multiply the result by the original number we get what is called the cube of the original number. This process is called cubing the number. The reverse process of finding the number which, when multiplied by itself and then by itself again, is equal to the given number, is called extracting the cube root of the given number. Thus, since 5 * 5 * 5 = 125, 125 is the cube of 5 and 5 is the cube root of 125.

To find the cube of any number on the slide rule set the indicator over the number on the D scale and read the answer on the K scale under the hair-line. To find the cube root of any number set the indicator over the number on the K scale and read the answer on the D scale under the hair-line. Just as on the A scale, where there were two places where you could set a given number, on the K scale there are three places where a number may be set. To tell which of the three to use, we must make use of the following rule.

(a) If the number is greater than one. For 1, 4, 7, 10, etc., digits to the left of the decimal point, use the left-hand third of the K scale. For 2, 5, 8, 11, etc., digits to the left of the decimal point, use the middle third of the K scale. For 3, 6, 9, 12, etc., digits to the left of the decimal point use the right-hand third of the K scale.

(b) If the number is less than one. We now tell which scale to use by counting the number of zeros to the right of the decimal point before the first digit not zero. If there are 2, 5, 8, 11, etc., zeros, use the left-hand third of the K scale. If there are 1, 4, 7, 10, etc., zeros, then use the middle third of the K scale. If there are no zeros or 3, 6, 9, 12, etc., zeros, then use the right-hand third of the K scale. For example:

Example 41: cube_root(185) = 5.70

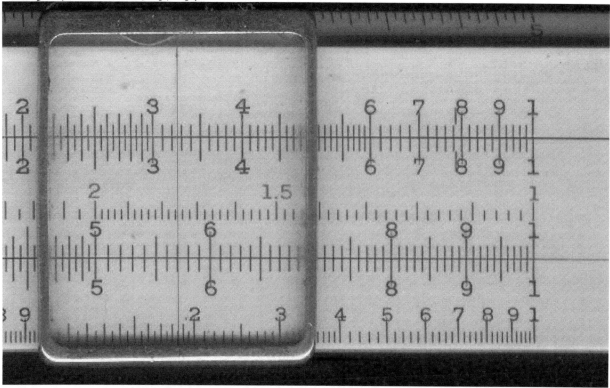

Since there are 3 digits in the given number, we set the indicator on 185 in the right-hand third of the K scale, and read the result 570 on the D scale. We can place the decimal point by thinking of the nearest perfect cube, which is 125. Therefore, the decimal point must be placed so as to give 5.70, which is nearest to 5, the cube root of 125.

Example 42: cube_root(.034) = .324

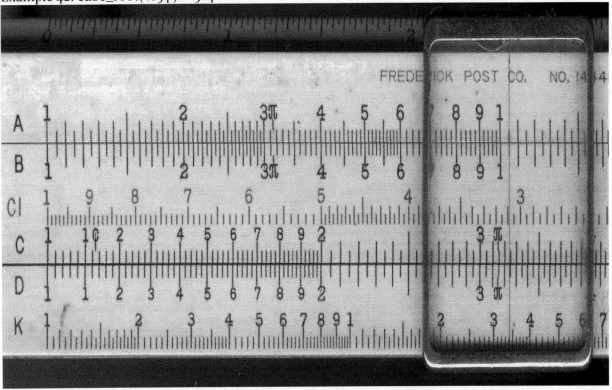

Since there is one zero between the decimal point and the first digit not zero, we must set the indicator over 34 on the middle third of the K scale. We read the result 324 on the D scale. The decimal point may be placed as follows:

cube_root(.034) = cube_root(34/1000) = 1/10 cube_root(34)

The nearest perfect cube to 34 is 27, so our answer must be close to one-tenth of the cube root of 27 or nearly 0.3. Therefore, we must place the decimal point to give 0.324. A group of examples for practice in extraction of cube root follows:

Example 43: cube_root(64) = 4

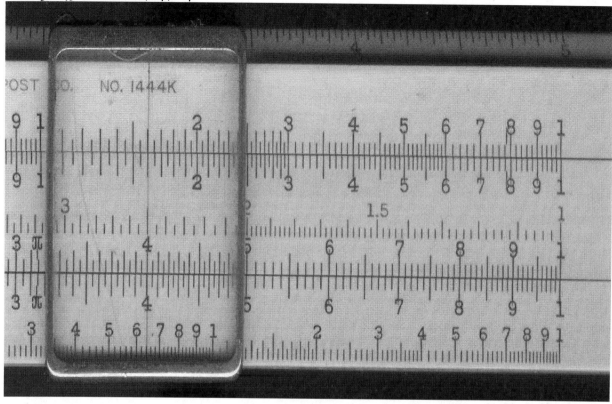

44: cube_root(8) = 2

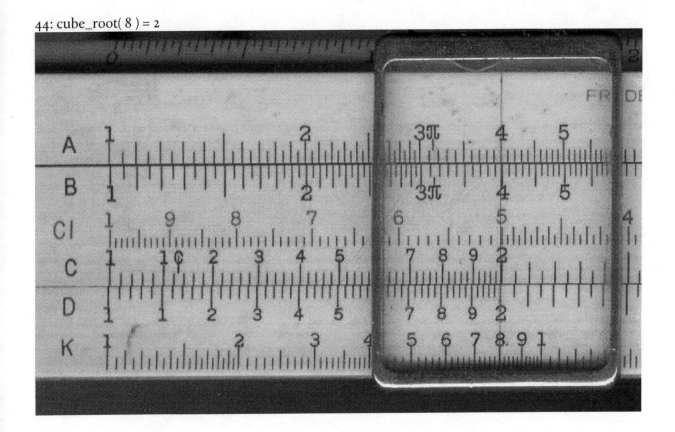

45: cube_root(343) = 7

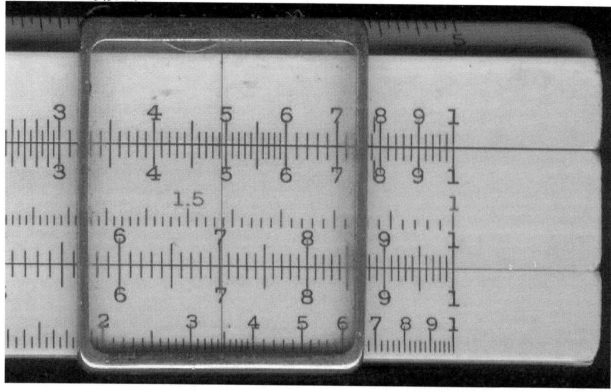

46: cube_root(.000715) = .0894

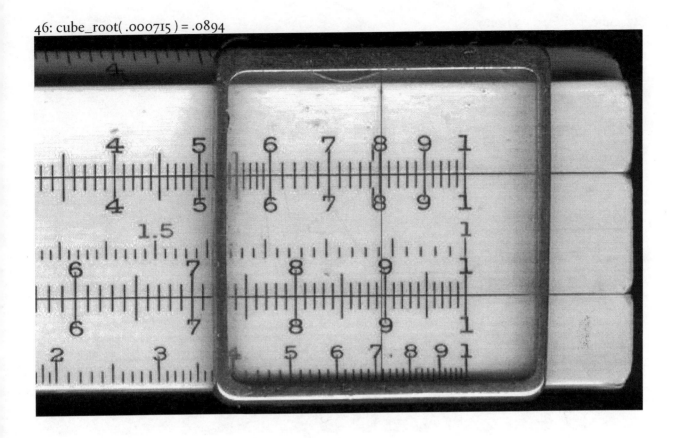

47: cube_root(.00715) = .193

48: cube_root(.0715) = .415

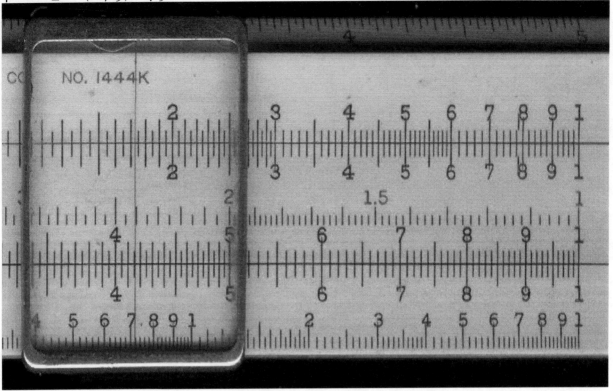

49: cube_root(.516) = .803

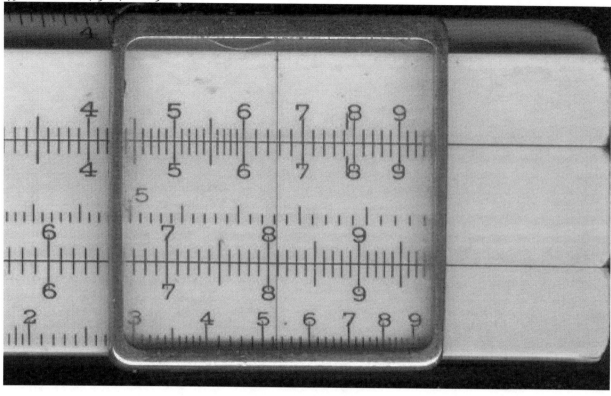

50: cube_root(27.8) = 3.03

51: cube_root(5.49) = 1.76

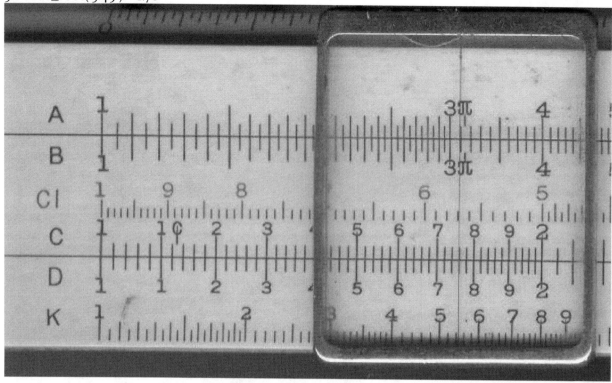

52: cube_root(87.1) = 4.43

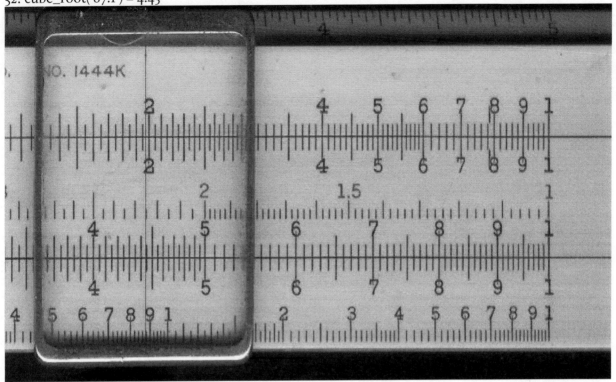

THE 1.5 AND 2/3 POWER

If the indicator is set over a given number on the A scale, the number under the hair-line on the K scale is the 1.5 power of the given number. If the indicator is set over a given number on the K scale, the number under the hair-line on the A scale is the 2/3 power of the given number.

4 to the 3/2 power is 8 8 to the 2/3 power is 4.

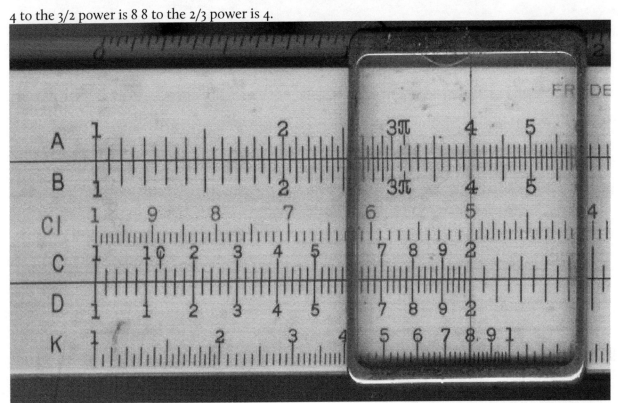

COMBINATIONS OF PROCESSES

A slide rule is especially useful where some combination of processes is necessary, like multiplying 3 numbers together and dividing by a third. Operations of this sort may be performed in such a way that the final answer is obtained immediately without finding intermediate results.

1. Multiplying several numbers together. For example, suppose it is desired to multiply 4 * 8 * 6. Place the right-hand index of the C scale over 4 on the D scale and set the indicator over 8 on the C scale. Now, leaving the indicator where it is, move the slider till the right-hand index is under the hairline. Now, leaving the slider where it is, move the indicator until it is over 6 on the C scale, and read the result, 192, on the D scale. This may be continued indefinitely, and so as many numbers as desired may be multiplied together.

Example 53: 2.32 * 154 * .0375 * .56 = 7.54

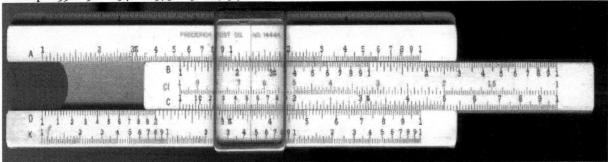

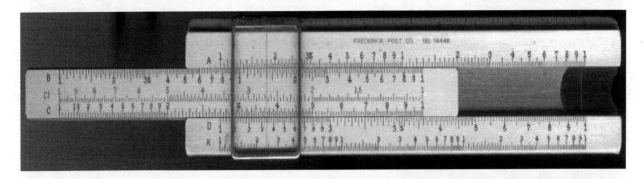

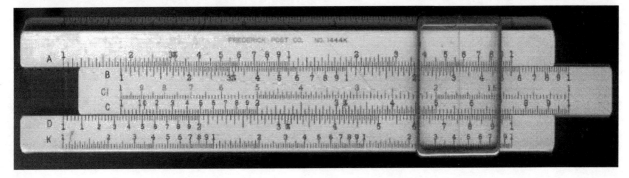

2. Multiplication and division. Suppose we wish to do the following example:

Example 54: (4 * 15) / 2.5 = 24

First divide 4 by 2.5. Set indicator over 4 on the D scale and move the slider until 2.5 is under the hairline. The result of this division, 1.6, appears under the left-hand index of the C scale. We do not need to write it down, however, but we can immediately move the indicator to 15 on the C scale and read the final result 24 on the D scale under the hair-line. Let us consider a more complicated problem of the same type:

Example 55: (30/7.5) * (2/4) * (4.5/5) * (1.5/3) = .9

First set indicator over 30 on the D scale and move slider until 7.5 on the C scale comes under the hairline. The intermediate result, 4, appears under the right-hand index of the C scale. We do not need to write it down but merely note it by moving the indicator until the hair-line is over the right-hand index of the C scale. Now we want to multiply this result by 2, the next factor in the numerator. Since two is out beyond the body of the rule, transfer the slider till the other (left-hand) index of the C scale is under the hair-line, and then move the indicator to 2 on the C scale. Thus, successive division and multiplication is continued until all the factors have been used. The order in which the factors are taken does not affect the result. With a little practice you will learn to take them in the order which will require the fewest settings. The following examples are for practice:

Example 56: (6/3.5) * (4/5) * (3.5/2.4) * (2.8/7) = .8

Example 57: 352 * (273/254) * (760/768) = 374

An alternative method of doing these examples is to proceed exactly as though you were multiplying all the factors together, except that whenever you come to a number in the denominator you use the CI scale instead of the C scale. The reader is advised to practice both methods and use whichever one he likes best.

3. The area of a circle. The area of a circle is found by multiplying 3.1416=PI by the square of the radius or by one-quarter the square of the diameter

Formula: A = PI * square(R) A = PI * (square(D) / 4)

Example 58: The radius of a circle is 0.25 inches; find its area.

Area = PI * square(0.25) = 0.196 square inches.

Set left-hand index of C scale over 0.25 on D scale. square(0.25) now appears above the left-hand index of the B scale. This can be multiplied by PI by moving the indicator to PI on the B scale and reading the answer .196 on the A scale. This is an example where it is convenient to multiply with the A and B scales.

Example 59: The diameter of a circle is 8.1 feet. What is its area?

Area = (PI / 4) * square(8.1)   = .7854 * square(8.1)   = 51.7 sq. inches.

Set right-hand index of the C scale over 8.1 on the D scale. Move the indicator till hair-line is over .7854 (the special long mark near 8) at the right hand of the B scale. Read the answer under the hair-line on the A scale. Another way of finding the area of a circle is to set 7854 on the B scale to one of the indices of the A scale, and read the area from the B scale directly above the given diameter on the D scale.

4. The circumference of a circle. Set the index of the B scale to the diameter and read the answer on the A scale opposite PI on the B scale

Formula: C = PI * D   C = 2 * PI * R

Example 60: The diameter of a circle is 1.54 inches, what is its circumference?

Set the left-hand index of the B scale to 1.54 on the A scale. Read the circumference 4.85 inches above PI on the B scale.

EXAMPLES FOR PRACTICE

61: What is the area of a circle 32-1/2 inches in diameter? Answer 830 sq. inches

62: What is the area of a circle 24 inches in diameter? Answer 452 sq. inches

63: What is the circumference of a circle whose diameter is 95 feet? Answer 298 ft.

64: What is the circumference of a circle whose diameter is 3.65 inches? Answer 11.5 inches

5. Ratio and Proportion.

Example 65:   3 : 7 : : 4 : X or (3/7) = (4/x) Find X

Set 3 on C scale over 7 on D scale. Read X on D scale under 4 on C scale. In fact, any number on the C scale is to the number directly under it on the D scale as 3 is to 7.

PRACTICAL PROBLEMS SOLVED BY SLIDE RULE

1. Discount. A firm buys a typewriter with a list price of $150, subject to a discount of 20% and 10%. How much does it pay?

A discount of 20% means 0.8 of the list price, and 10% more means 0.8 X 0.9 X 150 = 108.

To do this on the slide rule, put the index of the C scale opposite 8 on the D scale and move the indicator to 9 on the C scale. Then move the slider till the right-hand index of the C scale is under the hairline. Now, move the indicator to 150 on the C scale and read the answer $108 on the D scale. Notice that in this, as in many practical problems, there is no question about where the decimal point should go.

2. Sales Tax.

A man buys an article worth $12 and he must pay a sales tax of 1.5%. How much does he pay? A tax of 1.5% means he must pay 1.015 * 12.00.

Set index of C scale at 1.015 on D scale. Move indicator to 12 on C scale and read the answer $12.18 on the D scale.

A longer but more accurate way is to multiply 12 * .015 and add the result to $12.

3. Unit Price.

A motorist buys 17 gallons of gas at 19.5 cents per gallon. How much does he pay?

Set index of C scale at 17 on D scale and move indicator to 19.5 on C scale and read the answer $3.32 on the D scale.

4. Gasoline Mileage.

An automobile goes 175 miles on 12 gallons of gas. What is the average gasoline consumption?

Set indicator over 175 on D scale and move slider till 12 is under hair-line. Read the answer 14.6 miles per gallon on the D scale under the left-hand index of the C scale.

5. Average Speed.

A motorist makes a trip of 256 miles in 7.5 hours. What is his average speed?

Set indicator over 256 on D scale. Move slider till 7.5 on the C scale is under the hair-line. Read the answer 34.2 miles per hour under the right-hand index of the C scale.

6. Decimal Parts of an Inch.

What is 5/16 of an inch expressed as decimal fraction?

Set 16 on C scale over 5 on D scale and read the result .3125 inches on the D scale under the left-hand index of the C scale.

7. Physics.

A certain quantity of gas occupies 1200 cubic centimeters at a temperature of 15 degrees C and 740 millimeters pressure. What volume does it occupy at 0 degrees C and 760 millimeters pressure?

Volume = 1200 X (740/760) * (273/288) = 1100 cubic cm.

Set 760 on C scale over 12 on D scale. Move indicator to 740 on C scale. Move slider till 288 on C scale is under hair-line. Move indicator to 273 on C scale. Read answer, 1110, under hair-line on D scale.

8. Chemistry.

How many grams of hydrogen are formed when 80 grams of zinc react with sufficient hydrochloric acid to dissolve the metal?

(80 / X) = (65.4 / 2.01)

Set 65.4 on C scale over 2.01 on D scale. Read X = 2.46 grams under 80 on C scale.

In conclusion, we want to impress upon those to whom the slide rule is a new method of doing their mathematical calculations, and also the experienced operator of a slide rule, that if they will form a habit of, and apply themselves to, using a slide rule at work, study, or during recreations, they will be well rewarded in the saving of time and energy. ALWAYS HAVE YOUR SLIDE RULE AND INSTRUCTION BOOK WITH YOU, the same as you would a fountain pen or pencil.

The present day wonders of the twentieth century prove that there is no end to what an individual can accomplish--the same applies to the slide rule.

You will find after practice that you will be able to do many specialized problems that are not outlined in this instruction book. It depends entirely upon your ability to do what we advocate and to be slide-rule conscious in all your mathematical problems.

CONVERSION FACTORS

1. Length

1 mile = 5280 feet = 1760 yards

1 inch = 2.54 centimeters

1 meter = 39.37 inches

2. Weight (or Mass)

1 pound = 16 ounces = 0.4536 kilograms

1 kilogram = 2.2 pounds

1 long ton = 2240 pounds

1 short ton = 2000 pounds

3. Volume

1 liquid quart = 0.945 litres

1 litre = 1.06 liquid quarts

1 U. S. gallon = 4 quarts = 231 cubic inches

4. Angular Measure

3.14 radians = PI radians = 180 degrees

1 radian = 57.30 degrees

5. Pressure

760 millimeters of mercury = 14.7 pounds per square inch

6. Power

1 horse power = 550 foot pounds per second = 746 watts

7. Miscellaneous

60 miles per hour = 88 feet per second

980 centimeters per second per second = 32.2 feet per second per second = acceleration of gravity.

1 cubic foot of water weighs 62.4 pounds

1 gallon of water weighs 8.34 pounds

Made in the USA
Monee, IL
12 December 2024

73409636R00042